"Goalie?" Ben couldn't believe where Coach Patty had assigned him to play. This was the play-offs. Ben was a goal scorer. But Coach wanted him to start the game as goalkeeper.

Ben had only played goalie a few times this season, and not for very long. Still, he'd stopped all but one shot.

So Ben grabbed the big yellow jersey and pulled it over his blue Bobcats shirt. He picked up the goalie gloves and stretched them onto his hands. Now there was even more pressure on him. If the Falcons jumped to a quick lead, it would be his fault.

This was *not* just another game.

By Rich Wallace for younger readers:

Sports Camp

Kickers
#1: The Ball Hogs
#2: Fake Out
#3: Benched
#4: Game-Day Jitters

KICKERS

Book 4

GAME-DAY JITTERS

by Rich Wallace

illustrated by Jimmy Holder

A Yearling Book

Text copyright © 2011 by Rich Wallace
Cover art and interior illustrations copyright © 2011 by Jimmy Holder

Visit us on the Web! www.randomhouse.com/kids

Educators and librarians, for a variety of teaching tools, visit us at www.randomhouse.com/teachers

The Library of Congress has cataloged the hardcover edition of this work as follows:
Wallace, Rich.
Kickers : game-day jitters / Rich Wallace ; [illustrated by Jimmy Holder].
p. cm.
Summary: With help from his older brother Larry, nine-year-old Ben learns to cope with his nervousness about the Kickers League playoffs. Includes "Ben's Top Ten Tips for Soccer Players."
ISBN 978-0-375-85757-7 (trade) — ISBN 978-0-375-95757-4 (lib. bdg.) —
ISBN 978-0-375-89710-8 (ebook)
[1. Worry—Fiction. 2. Competition (Psychology)—Fiction. 3. Soccer—Fiction.
4. Brothers—Fiction.] I. Holder, Jimmy, ill. II. Title. III. Title: Game-day jitters.
PZ7.W15877Kig 2011
[Fic]—dc22
2010004081

ISBN 978-0-375-85095-0 (pbk.)

Printed in the United States of America
10 9 8 7 6 5 4 3 2

First Yearling Edition 2012

THE BOBCATS
Team Roster

Ben

Mark

Erin

Shayna

Omar

Jordan

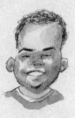

Darren

Kim

Coach Patty

CHAPTER ONE
A Painful Memory

Ben was reading at his desk when a wad of paper hit him in the chin. The paper fell to the floor and Ben turned to glare at his classmate Loop.

Loop was laughing. He mouthed the word "goal" at Ben and looked away.

Ben reached out with his foot and snagged the paper, sweeping it toward him. He glanced at the front of the room, but the teacher hadn't

noticed anything. They were supposed to be reading silently for ten minutes.

Ben picked up the paper and carefully unfolded it. He could tell that several of the kids nearby were looking at him, but Mrs. Soto seemed unaware.

He flattened the paper out on his desk and read it.

PREDICTED SCORES:

Rabbits 2, Panthers 1

Falcons 6, Bobcats 0

Ben looked over at Loop and shook his head. "No way," he mouthed.

Loop patted his chest twice and smirked. Then he nodded. He was confident and he had a right to be. The Falcons were by far the hottest soccer team in the Kickers League.

But the Bobcats—Ben's team—were pretty hot, too. They'd won four out of their last five games and qualified for the play-offs. On Thursday afternoon, they'd be facing the Falcons in the semifinals. The winner of that match would play in the championship game on Saturday.

Ben winced as he thought about the first game between the Bobcats and the Falcons. That had been several weeks ago. At that point in the season, the Falcons hadn't won a single game. But things started to click for them against the Bobcats, and the game turned into a rout. Loop and his teammate Alex did all the scoring in a 3–0 shutout.

The memory of that game had stayed with Ben ever since. He and Loop were friendly rivals in most sports and games. Loop definitely had the upper hand lately.

The Falcons had won all of their games since then, usually by big margins. Most of the players in the league thought the Falcons would end up as the champions.

Not me, Ben thought. *Their season ends tomorrow.*

"All right, class," said Mrs. Soto, standing at her desk. "Get ready for recess."

"Yes!" said Loop, who was always ready to play.

Ben didn't say anything, but he was relieved

to be getting a break. He was a good student, but sitting still all morning made him fidgety. He couldn't wait to get outside.

Loop caught up to Ben as they walked along the hallway. "What do you think of my predictions?" he asked.

Ben rolled his eyes. "I agree that the Rabbits will probably beat the Panthers," he said. "But you're dreaming if you think you guys will shut us out again."

"We'll see who's dreaming tomorrow," Loop replied. "We've scored twenty-four goals over the past six games, and we've only given up three. How does your team compare?"

Ben did some quick addition in his head as they stepped onto the playground. In six games, the Bobcats had scored ten goals and given up nine. But if you didn't count the loss to the Falcons, the past five weeks looked pretty good.

"We never score a lot of goals," Ben said, "but we score enough to win. And we're a *lot* better than the last time we played you."

The other fourth-grade classes were already on the playground. Loop jogged over to the four-square courts. One of the players tossed him a ball and Loop juggled it with his thighs, bouncing it back and forth like a soccer ball.

Ben sat on the edge of a seesaw, straddling the green board and watching Loop.

Loop turned to Ben and waved his hand toward the court. "You playing?"

Ben shook his head. "Not today."

"How come?"

"I'm saving my energy."

Loop smiled. "It won't help. We'll thrash you tomorrow no matter how much energy you have."

You wait, Ben thought. He knew that the Bobcats had made a huge improvement over the past few games. But he also knew how good Loop's team was. They were fast and skilled, and they played a smart style of soccer. Beating them would be incredibly hard.

Ben jumped a little as the seesaw shook. He glanced over his shoulder and saw his best friend and teammate Erin pushing the other end.

"Earth to Ben," Erin said.

Ben stood carefully so the seesaw wouldn't rise up and smack him. "Thinking about tomorrow," he said.

"The big game," Erin said cheerfully. She was an excellent soccer player, but she never seemed to take the games as seriously as Ben did. He knew that he sometimes took the games *too* seriously, and that had caused some trouble. He'd been kicked out of one game and suspended for another. He'd worked hard on controlling his temper since then.

"I heard Loop bragging again," Erin said with a laugh.

"He was mouthing off about the game," Ben said. "Thinks they're going to beat us, like, a hundred to nothing."

"He's just trying to throw off your concentration," Erin said. "Don't let him get to you."

"He won't." Ben took the crumpled-up paper out of his pocket and showed it to Erin. "He'll eat this tomorrow after we beat them."

Erin looked at the paper. "Six–nothing?" she said.

"That's what he wrote. Come on, I need to burn off some steam. Let's shoot baskets."

They walked across the playground and Ben picked up a basketball. He dribbled a few times, then charged toward the basket and made a layup. He didn't really need to save energy—he just didn't want to listen to Loop any longer. Ben *never* ran out of energy.

"One-on-one?" he asked, dribbling the basketball steadily.

Erin swiped out her hand and stole the ball. "Nah," she said as she darted away. "Let's play HORSE."

Ben frowned but said, "Okay." He'd rather compete in a real game, but HORSE would do for now. "Go ahead."

Erin dribbled to the free-throw line, took one step back, and shot a jumper. The ball banked off the backboard and into the hoop.

"You didn't call a bank," Ben said. "So I don't have to."

Erin shrugged. "Bank or not, you still have to make the shot."

Ben eyed the basket, then jumped and shot. The ball rolled around the rim but fell out.

"That's an *H*," Erin said.

"No kidding."

Erin did a simple layup from the right, and Ben matched it. She missed her next shot, and Ben made one.

By the time recess ended, both of them had reached H-O-R-S.

"We'll finish this tomorrow," Ben said.

"Fair enough," Erin replied. "But I get the first shot."

Ben wiped his forehead with his hand. He'd broken a sweat, which was always a good thing as far as he was concerned. He felt good now, ready for the rest of the school day. He couldn't even remember why he'd been so keyed up before recess.

But then he saw Loop and he remembered. Soccer. Tomorrow afternoon. The play-offs.

* * *

"This is quite a sports week in our house," Ben's dad said at dinner that night.

Ben pushed a pile of string beans with his fork and stared at the chicken. He hadn't eaten anything yet. He was too nervous about tomorrow's game.

Across the table, his older brother, Larry, had a mouthful of food and was grinning as he chewed.

He won't be so hungry tomorrow night, Ben thought. *Before his race.*

Larry would be competing in the league cross-country championship race on Friday afternoon. He was one of the best runners on the Lincoln Junior High School team.

"Eat up, Ben," Mom said.

"I'm not hungry."

Mom set down her fork. "You're *never* not hungry," she said. "What's the matter?"

"He's too worked up about tomorrow," Larry

said. "Listen, Ben. It's just another game."

"It's *not* 'just another game,'" Ben snapped. "This is the play-offs."

Larry shook his head slowly. "My coach always tells us to prepare for every race the same way."

"This isn't a race." Ben stabbed the chicken and left the fork standing straight up in it. "We're playing the best team in the league. The loser is done for the season."

"You have to focus," Larry said. "Of course you'll play harder than ever. Championship games are like that. But you'll do better if you start out by telling yourself that it's just another game."

Ben scowled and yanked the fork out of the chicken. He took a swig of milk and set down the glass. "You wouldn't say the league championship is just another *race*, would you?"

Larry shrugged. "That *is* what I'm saying. If I let myself get all nervous about it, I'd probably run badly. Staying focused and calm is the way to go."

"Easy for you to say," Ben replied. "Let's see how you feel tomorrow night. Or on Friday before the race."

Larry laughed. "You're right. It isn't easy to stay calm. But you can try. And believe me, you'll be sorry tomorrow if you don't eat. You'll be sprinting around that soccer field harder than ever, and you'll run out of fuel."

Ben scooped up a bite of chicken and shoved it into his mouth. It tasted good. Suddenly he realized how hungry he was. He ate everything on his plate and then asked for more.

* * *

Ben lay on his bed later that evening, staring at the ceiling. He thought about the first time his team had played the Falcons. Loop and his teammate Alex had made Ben look silly a few times with some very tricky fakes. He'd worked on that a lot since then—making fakes of his own and learning not to get fooled by another player's moves.

And even though the Bobcats had lost that game, Ben knew his team was nearly as good as the Falcons. They could keep the game close tomorrow. But could they beat them? He wasn't so sure about that. And if he played poorly, the game could be a blowout.

Ben's door was open, but Larry knocked on it to get his attention. "How you doing, knucklehead?" Larry said.

"I'm okay. Just nervous."

"I didn't mean to make you feel bad before,"

Larry said. "I just know what it's like to get so worked up before a game that you hurt your chances. The other team will be jittery, too."

"Loop doesn't get the jitters," Ben said. "He acts like they've already won the game."

"Then he'll be shocked if you guys jump out to the lead tomorrow," Larry said. "Let him think they're going to stomp on you again. Being overconfident can be even worse than being afraid."

"I'm not afraid," Ben said. "I just can't wait to get going. I want to win this game more than any I've ever played."

CHAPTER TWO
Full Force

___

As soon as the final bell rang on Thursday, Ben hurried out of the classroom and out of the school. He was already wearing his soccer shirt, and he had his shorts on under his pants. His shin guards and cleats were in his backpack, so he ran all the way to the field.

He had planned to sit in the bleachers and watch the first play-off game between the Rabbits and the Panthers, but he couldn't sit still.

He kicked a ball back and forth with Erin for a few minutes, then dropped to the grass and looked up at the clouds. The air was cool and there was a light wind. A perfect day for soccer.

Once in a while, Ben heard cheering from the field, so he looked over. Usually it was the Rabbits who were cheering.

He stood near the sidelines to watch the end of the game. The Rabbits had beaten Ben's team both times they'd played. Ben knew they'd have a third meeting if the Bobcats could beat the Falcons, because the Rabbits were on their way to an easy win over the Panthers.

First things first, he thought. This semifinal would be the Bobcats' toughest test yet.

When the game ended, Ben stayed put for a minute, watching Loop and his teammates as they raced onto the field in their red jerseys. They sure looked confident.

Ben looked around at his own teammates. The Bobcats had started the season slowly, not even scoring a goal until their third game. But they'd become a solid team in the second half of the season.

We've come a long way, he thought. He swallowed hard. Could they really beat the Falcons? Or would this game be as embarrassing as the last time they'd played?

Mark and Kim were passing a ball around. Ben had had some trouble with Mark early on, but once they'd started working together on the field, they'd begun to get along off it, too. Kim was a great passer, and she and Ben had combined on a few scoring plays.

Over by the goal, Jordan and Erin were firing shots toward Shayna. Jordan had probably made the most improvement of all the Bobcats. He'd scored quite a few times.

Ben noticed that Shayna was limping a bit.

He stepped over to the side of the field and nodded to Omar and Darren, who were just arriving.

"Huge game!" said Omar, raising his palm for Ben to smack it.

"You don't have to remind me," Ben said. "I haven't stopped thinking about this one since last Saturday."

Ben ran back and forth across the field a few times, then started dribbling a ball. He felt loose and excited.

Loop can think whatever he wants, Ben told himself. *This is going to be a close game.*

"Goalie?" Ben couldn't believe where Coach Patty had assigned him to play. This was the play-offs. Ben was a goal scorer. But Coach wanted him to start the game as goalkeeper.

"How come?" he asked.

"I think it's our best chance," Coach said, taking Ben aside from the rest of the team. "Shayna usually plays goalie for the first half, but her left ankle is sore. Let's see how she feels after playing defense for a while. She might be ready to take over as keeper later."

Ben nodded. Goalkeepers had to dart from side to side and jump a lot. A sore ankle would be a problem.

Coach smiled. "She keeps telling me she's okay, but I can tell." Shayna was Coach Patty's daughter.

"But why me?" Ben asked. There were six other Bobcats besides him and Shayna.

"The Falcons will be coming at us full force at the beginning," Coach said. "I don't want them to get a quick lead. You've done very well when you've played goalie. Don't worry— you'll play up front before long."

"Okay," Ben said.

Coach was probably right. With Loop and Alex on the front line at the start, the Falcons were likely to bombard whoever was in goal for the Bobcats. Ben had played goalie only a few times this season, and not for very long. Still, he'd stopped all but one shot.

So Ben grabbed the big yellow jersey and pulled it over his blue Bobcats shirt. He picked up the goalie gloves and stretched them onto his hands. Now there was even more pressure on him. If the Falcons jumped to a quick lead, it would be his fault.

This was *not* just another game.

His teammates shot the ball at him several times, and Ben caught every shot or knocked it away. Mark sent a hard one toward the upper corner of the goal, but Ben leaped and tipped it over the crossbar.

"Looking good," Mark said.

"I'm ready."

"Huddle up, team!" Coach called. Ben jogged out toward the center circle, and the rest of the Bobcats gathered around him.

"Be aggressive, but be smart," Coach said. "When we have the ball, spread out. When they have the ball, cover them."

Ben stuck out his hand and Erin set hers on top. The rest of the teammates stacked theirs in the pile, too, and Ben said, "Three . . . two . . . one . . ."

"Bobcats!" they yelled.

As the huddle broke, Ben leaped into the air, kicking himself in the butt with both feet. *Let's get this thing started*, he thought.

He looked across the field and saw Loop staring back. Loop patted himself on the chest and pointed at Ben.

Yes, the Falcons would be coming at them with full force.

CHAPTER THREE
Making Some Luck

As he walked toward the goal, Ben tucked the goalie jersey into his shorts. It was baggy and long. He clapped his hands and said, "Let's go," but he wasn't feeling confident.

He could see his parents and Larry sitting in the bleachers with several other adults. Many of the kids from the teams who hadn't made the play-offs were here, too. And the Rabbits were all on the other side of the field, watching with some of the Panthers. This crowd was far bigger than at any of the Bobcats' previous games. More people to watch him mess up.

Tune it out, Ben thought. *Focus on stopping Loop and Alex*. He took a deep breath and tried to relax.

When the game began, Ben could tell that his coach had been right. The Falcons quickly moved the ball toward the Bobcats' goal, with Loop and Alex controlling most of the action.

When Erin finally knocked the ball out of bounds, Loop raced to the sideline for a corner kick.

Ben raised his hands and let out his breath, ready to catch the ball or dive at it. Alex was crouched in front of the goal, and players from both teams were packed in tight.

Ben glanced at Alex, who looked ready to

spring into the air. Loop would be lofting the ball in front of him, hoping Alex could head it into the net.

"Get up high," Ben said, catching Erin's attention.

As Loop stepped forward to kick the ball, Alex drifted back. The ball was coming toward him. Erin and Mark leaped for it, too, but Alex got higher and met it with his forehead, thrusting it toward the corner of the goal.

Ben dived and got a hand on it, but the ball spun to the side. Loop had sprinted toward the goal and reached the ball first. Without breaking stride, he pounded it at the goal. It flew on a line drive about a foot above the ground.

Still on his knees, Ben caught the ball and rolled.

"Great save," said Jordan.

Ben could hear shouts of approval from the bleachers, too.

He leaped to his feet and stepped forward to punt the ball, but then he had a better thought. All of the Bobcats were still near this goal, so booting the ball way up the field would give it to one of the Falcons' defensive players. Instead, Ben flung the ball toward Mark, who was running toward the sideline. Mark fielded the pass and sprinted ahead of all but the two Falcon defenders.

"Breakaway!" Ben yelled, watching as Mark raced up the field.

Loop and Alex and the others were in pursuit, but Mark dodged past one defender and headed for the other end of the field. He was fast, and he'd become a very good dribbler over the course of the season.

Jordan had outrun most of the Falcons and was approaching the goal. Mark made one more dodge to swing past the last Falcon defender, then sent a crisp pass across the front of the goal. Jordan was there, and he skillfully knocked the ball past the goalie and into the net.

"Unbelievable!" Ben yelled. They were less than a minute into the game, and the Bobcats already had the lead.

Loop was standing near midfield with his mouth open, staring toward the Falcons' goal. He stepped over to Alex and said something Ben couldn't hear. Alex nodded.

"How's the ankle?" Ben called to Shayna.

"A little sore," she said. "I think I'll be all right."

"That's good." Now that the Bobcats were in front, maybe Coach would take Ben out of the goalie position.

But that didn't happen. The next time the ball went out of bounds, Coach sent Omar onto the field to replace Shayna. She was limping more than before. Ben watched as she took a seat on the bench and pulled off her left shoe.

A shout took Ben's attention back to the field. Loop was racing down the sideline with the ball, and Alex was cutting across the middle. Omar seemed confused and was running toward Loop, leaving the front of the goal wide open.

"Drop back!" Ben called. "Don't abandon me."

Erin had come back from midfield and moved toward Alex. Omar hustled over, too. Ben knew that Loop and Alex always looked for each other first before passing to their other teammates.

Mark had cut off Loop's path and Jordan had him trapped. Loop had no choice but to pass the ball back to a different Falcon.

Loop stood still for a second while Mark and Jordan started chasing the ball. But then he took off like a bolt of lightning, cutting behind the defenders. The ball went to Alex, who sliced it toward Loop. Loop fielded the ball at full speed and raced straight toward the goal.

Ben crouched low, ready to dive at the ball when Loop shot. He took a few steps forward, hoping to force Loop to the side. But Loop kept running straight.

"Where's my help?" Ben called, never taking his eyes away from Loop.

Alex had charged forward, too, and he was a step ahead of Erin and Omar. Loop passed the ball, and Alex shot.

The ball was waist-high, zinging toward the goal. Ben dived, and the ball skidded off his hand and whacked him in the shoulder. It bounced toward Loop, near the corner of the goal. Ben leaped to his feet, closing off the side of the net.

It was a tough angle to shoot from, but Loop

was very skilled. He shot the ball hard, and it nicked the goalpost. Players scrambled around as the ball took a wild bounce.

Jordan swooped in and kicked the ball hard, clearing it away from the goal. It went out of bounds near the corner of the field.

"Lucky break!" Loop said, frowning at Ben. "That shot just missed."

Ben looked away. The Falcons had already put the ball in play with a throw-in.

"Get out there!" Ben called to Omar and Erin. They'd stayed near the goal, leaving a few players open. The ball was crossed to Alex, who trapped it with his foot, stepped forward, and shot from twenty yards out.

Ben easily caught the ball. This time he punted it, and it sailed in the air past midfield. Blue- and red-shirted players ran after it.

"Way to go, Ben!" Shayna yelled from the sideline.

Ben nodded, but he kept his eyes on the field. That flurry of shots had tired everyone out. The pace of the game began to slow for a few moments.

The slow pace didn't last long. Alex and Loop led another burst toward the Bobcats' goal. Ben knocked down one shot and caught another. He was fired up now.

Nothing gets past me, he thought. *Loop will look like a real jerk when this one ends.*

"You must be the luckiest guy on the planet," Loop said as Ben lined up the ball at the edge of the goal box to kick it back into play.

"I make my own luck," Ben said.

"We should have three goals by now," Loop replied.

"What a shame," Ben said. "Are those real tears?"

The referee had jogged over. "What's the problem here?" he asked.

"No problem," Ben said. "At least not for me."

"Then put the ball in play," the ref said.

Ben raced forward and kicked it long and hard. Jordan was the first one to it, and he dribbled up the field, making a nice fake to get past a defender.

Loop ran after the ball, too. Ben couldn't help but smile.

Keep him frustrated, he thought. *Take away his concentration, just like he tries to do to you.*

Coach made the right choice putting me in goal. They probably would have two or three goals by now if I wasn't here.

But there was a long way to go in this game. And Loop was racing down the field toward the goal again.

CHAPTER FOUR
Right Back at 'Em

When the first half ended, Ben jogged toward the Bobcats' bench. He was thrilled that his entire team ran over to meet him, slapping him on the back and shouting, "Great work!"

He'd lost count of all the shots he'd blocked or caught or knocked away. Probably close to a dozen. The Bobcats still held a 1–0 lead.

Ben picked up the bag of orange slices and

ripped into one with his teeth. The juice squirted down his chin.

"Halfway there!" Jordan said, giving Ben a light punch in the shoulder.

"You really shut them down, Ben," Erin said.

Ben smiled. "We shut them up, too."

Ben looked for Shayna. She was standing near her mom. "How is it?" Ben asked.

Shayna winced. She hadn't returned to the game. "Too sore," she said. "You were great, by the way."

"Thanks." He'd been hoping she'd play goalie in the second half, but the Bobcats had other options. Ben was just glad that he'd be playing up front again.

"Here's the lineup," Coach said. "Ben, Kim, Jordan on the front line. Omar and Mark on defense. Darren in goal."

Ben turned to Darren. "We'll keep 'em away from you."

"There's twenty minutes of soccer left," Coach said. "Don't go out there and try to protect the lead for the entire half. You need to stay on the attack. We need another goal or two."

Ben saw his brother and his parents walking over to him. Larry was carrying a bottle of water.

"That was some wild action, huh?" Larry said, handing the bottle to Ben.

"Brutal," Ben replied, shaking his head. "I was *really* focused on stopping the ball."

"Just another game, right?"

Ben gave a tight smile. "Sort of," he said. "I know what you mean, though. Don't let the pressure get to me."

"Are you still going to be the goalie?" Dad asked.

"No. Center forward."

"Still jittery?" Mom asked.

Ben shook his head. "I didn't have time to be nervous. Every time I looked up, the Falcons were shooting the ball at me."

As they lined up for the second half, Ben noticed that Loop and Alex were set up as defenders for the Falcons. But all that meant was that five Falcons would be attacking the goal, not just the three forwards. Loop and Alex were fast enough to get back on defense anytime the Bobcats had the ball.

Ben kept his eyes on Loop. Loop glanced over once, but he didn't do his usual showboat routine of patting his chest and pointing. He was very serious. When his eyes caught Ben's, Loop looked away.

Not so sure of yourself now, huh, Loop? Ben thought.

But the second half started much like the

first, with the Falcons controlling the ball and keeping it near the Bobcats' goal. Twice Mark kicked the ball away just as Alex was about to shoot. Darren made a couple of easy saves, too.

Midway through the half, Ben was staying close to Loop as the Falcons attacked. Jordan stole the ball for the Bobcats and kicked it forward, but the Falcons got it right back.

Everyone on the field had been running toward the Falcons' end, so the quick interception left Loop with some room. Alex's pass went to him, and Ben stumbled as he cut back to Loop.

Loop was angling toward the goal, and Ben raced over to force him away. Darren was in a good position to make a save, but Loop stopped short, made a couple of jukes, and faked his way past Ben.

"Here!" came a shout from near the goal. It was Alex, and he was wide open. Loop's pass found him perfectly. Darren dived at the ball, but it slipped through his hands and into the net. Alex had tied the score.

Ben felt a hard bump to his shoulder as Loop ran into him.

"Watch it," Ben mumbled.

Loop turned and snorted. "We burnt you that time," he said.

They'd kept the high-scoring Falcons scoreless for thirty minutes, but just like that the game was tied. Ben knew he hadn't been burned. He'd played good defense, but he couldn't cover Loop and Alex at the same time. Where had the rest of the Bobcats been?

Ben clapped his hands. "Let's get it right back!" he called. "Time to show some power."

The Bobcats hadn't had a scoring opportunity since that first goal, way back in the first minute of the game.

Coach sent Erin onto the field to replace

Omar. "You've got fresh legs," Ben said to her. "Let's run these guys off the field."

Mark jogged over to Ben. "I'm coming up on the attack," he said. "We need to apply some pressure."

Ben nodded and moved to the center circle to put the ball into play. He made a short pass to Kim, who turned and kicked it back to Mark.

Jordan was sprinting up one side of the field, with Ben running parallel to him in the center. Mark sent a long, high pass deep into the Falcons' end of the field. Alex got under it and trapped it with his thigh, then looked ahead for someone to pass to.

Ben could see where the ball would go. Loop was unguarded, but he was quite far down the field. Unless Alex passed the ball very hard, Ben would be able to get to it first.

Alex made a soft pass, rolling the ball along the turf toward Loop.

That's mine, Ben thought, racing toward it at full stride. He reached it half a step before Loop did.

With a quick pivot, Ben shielded the ball from Loop and took off toward the Falcons' goal. There were opponents in front of him, but Jordan was wide open to Ben's side. He yelled, "Support!" to let Ben know he was there.

Ben took two more strides, then slipped the ball to Jordan. Without slowing down, Ben curved behind the Falcons, who charged at Jordan.

Ben didn't even have to break stride as Jordan's pass headed between him and the goal. The goalie was ready to spring, but a quick shoulder fake from Ben sent him to the right.

Ben drove the ball hard to the left, and it lined into the back of the net.

The Bobcats had retaken the lead.

Ben made a fist and ran to Jordan, saying, "Fantastic pass!" They leaped and hit their chests together, then ran toward midfield.

Loop was standing alone, looking stunned. Ben had to go slightly out of his way to reach him, but he made a point of bumping Loop's shoulder with his own.

"Right back at you," Ben said. He didn't wait for Loop to respond, but kept running.

Ben glanced to the sideline and saw Coach gesturing for him to come over. Omar was running onto the field.

"I'm out?" Ben asked.

"Take a quick breather," Coach said. She set her hand on Ben's shoulder. "Two things to remember. First, keep your head together.

There was no need to bump into one of their players like that. You're lucky the referee didn't see it."

"Loop did the exact same thing to me."

"Just let it go. Second thing: I need you to go back to playing goalkeeper."

"Again?" Ben wiped his hands on his jersey. "I just scored!"

"Right. Which means if we can shut them out the rest of the way, we'll win."

"That's true," Ben said. But he wanted to be on that field, stealing the ball, making passes, taking another shot at the goal.

"Next time the ball goes out of bounds," Coach said, "go back in goal."

Ben paced the sideline, eager to get back on the field. Shayna hobbled over to him and pointed to her watch. "About six minutes to go," she said.

Within a minute, Mark had knocked the ball over the end line. Coach yelled, "Sub!" and Ben ran onto the field.

As the Falcons set up for a corner kick, Ben took the yellow jersey and the gloves from Darren. He jumped up and down a few times and stretched out his fingers. Then he sized up the players in front of the goal.

Alex and Loop were tucked in tight, waiting for the kick. Erin, Mark, and Jordan surrounded them.

"Clear that ball," Ben said to his teammates. "Kick it *away* from the goal."

Ben knew things would get wild on a corner kick. A shot could come from any angle.

And here it came. The kick was low, and Alex controlled it but was off balance. He turned and fired a shot, which bonked off the crossbar and bounced back onto the field. Mark kicked it away, but another Falcon trapped it with his chest and let it drop.

That player was a bit too eager, and he kicked the ball while it was still in the air. It flew over the goal.

Ben hustled back and grabbed the ball, setting it in the upper corner of the goal box. He scanned the field, then kicked the ball as hard as he could.

He hadn't hit the ball solidly, and it spun toward the side. A Falcon kicked it forward, and suddenly Loop and Mark were chasing it as it rolled quickly toward the goal.

Ben ran toward it, too. He shouted, "Keeper!" to let Mark know that he could get to it first and field it safely.

Mark backed off, but Loop kept running. Ben reached the ball just ahead of Loop and dived for it. They were inside the goal box, so Ben was allowed to use his hands. He cradled the ball in his arms and rolled, and Loop leaped over him, crashing to the ground, too.

Ben was up first, and he punted the ball long and high. As he watched it soar past midfield, he heard Loop say, "Get used to that ground. We'll be stomping you into it."

Ben ignored the taunting this time. He knew the Falcons would keep up the pressure until the final whistle.

CHAPTER FIVE
One-on-One

Ben had never felt so alert in his life. He could see every play developing; he knew which move the Falcons would make. He stopped every shot they took.

All the players on the field looked exhausted. But with less than two minutes remaining, they were using every ounce of energy they had left. The Bobcats weren't concerned with scoring again. All they had to do was preserve the 2–1 lead. The Falcons were frantic, though, chasing every loose ball and desperately trying to knot the game.

Here came Alex again, streaming down the sideline with the ball, dodging past Erin and then Jordan. He shifted left, then right, and passed to a teammate near the corner.

Ben saw Loop sprinting straight toward the goal. "Cover him!" he yelled.

Mark darted over, but Loop fielded the pass and pivoted to shoot. The ball careened off Mark's shin guard and wobbled toward the goal. Ben ran forward and smothered it.

He stood up and let out his breath. *No need to hurry*, he thought. Every second of delay was to his team's advantage. So he looked around the field.

Kim was alone near the sideline, and Ben rolled the ball hard toward her. She cut toward it and took off, covering a lot of ground before any of the Falcons caught up.

With a nifty move, Kim stopped short and flipped the ball to Mark. He booted it hard and chased it, sending it down near the Falcons' goal.

Ben pumped his fist as a Falcons defender knocked the ball out of bounds. Kim ran over to take the throw-in. The Bobcats were controlling the ball, and the clock was ticking away.

"Move up a little," Ben called to Omar, who was far back on defense. "Go to midfield. Keep the ball down that end."

Omar jogged forward a bit. Down the other end, Jordan had taken an off-balance shot that went out of bounds.

Ben hopped up and down. This game was nearly over. And what a job he'd done. He'd stopped every shot, and he'd scored a goal of his own. And his work might already be done. If his teammates could keep the ball up at the other end of the field, the Falcons wouldn't get another chance.

It looked like that might happen. Kim made a steal and controlled the ball for a few seconds. When the Falcons got it back, the Bobcats swarmed the ball and kept it from coming downfield.

With seconds remaining, Loop finally broke free. He kicked the ball past Jordan and took off at a full sprint. He crossed midfield, then turned it on even harder.

Omar stepped up and forced Loop to go wider. But Alex was racing down, too, and Loop sent the ball directly into his path.

Ben dug in and crouched, ready to leap for the ball. It would be a tough shot for Alex; Ben had the corner of the goal protected.

Loop had cut back toward the middle, and Alex made the pass. Ben dodged that way.

As he lifted his leg to shoot, Loop suddenly fell forward, landing in a heap on the turf. Ben dived onto the loose ball. The referee blew his whistle.

Ben looked over. Mark was lying on the ground behind Loop. Loop sat up and groaned, rubbing his calf.

"That was a dangerous play," the referee said. "I'm awarding a penalty kick."

Penalty kicks were very rare in this league, but this one seemed to be justified. Mark had tripped Loop as he was about to shoot.

Mark shook his head, but he held out his hand for Loop and helped him to his feet.

"Here's the wrinkle," the referee continued. "Time has expired. So I want only the goalie and the shooter on the field. If the Falcons score, we go to overtime. If not, then the Bobcats win."

Ben looked at the sky and blew out his breath. Loop set the ball on the penalty mark, about twelve yards in front of the goal.

The referee explained the rule, since neither player had been involved in a penalty shot before.

"The goalie must stand still on the goal line

until the ball is kicked," he said. "The shooter can kick it only once. Since the game has ended, you can't score on a rebound, only on the first shot."

Loop stepped several feet back from the ball. Ben spread his arms a few inches from his hips and bent his knees. He could hear players from both teams yelling from the sidelines. It was just him and Loop. One-on-one.

Loop looked mean. Ben knew that he did, too. He'd made a lot of great saves today, but they'd be worth nothing if he didn't stop this shot.

He knew Loop would be aiming at a corner of the goal, but which one? If Ben guessed wrong and darted to one side, he'd leave the other side wide open. But would he be able to react quickly enough if he waited until the ball was in the air?

There was no more time to think. Loop charged forward and booted the ball. It soared to Ben's left, about shoulder height and fast.

Ben dived. He felt the ball strike his hands and he pushed hard.

As he hit the ground, Ben could hear the cheers. But who were they for? He looked back toward the goal and saw the ball, but it was *outside* the net.

Loop was squatting near the penalty line, his hands crossed behind his head, his eyes on the ground. The Bobcats were running toward Ben, leaping and shouting. He'd punched the ball over the goal. He'd made the save!

The next few minutes were wild, with players smacking him on the back, his parents and his brother giving him giant hugs, and his coach telling him he'd played the best game of his life.

The Bobcats crossed the field together and

shook hands with the Falcons. Alex smiled slightly as Ben took his hand. "Great save," he said.

Loop swung his hand and hit Ben's, but he kept walking away and didn't say a word. Ben let him go. He didn't need to speak to Loop. His play on the field had said it all.

CHAPTER SIX
Toughing It Out

Ben couldn't wait until recess the next day. Not because he wanted to burn off energy, but because he had a nice surprise for Loop.

He'd saved that paper with Loop's predictions on it. He planned to march over to Loop's four-square game and show it around.

Loop had been quiet all morning. Ben hadn't had a chance to talk to him before class. He did look over a couple of times and mimic

Loop's favorite gesture, patting himself on the chest and then pointing. Loop just frowned and looked away.

He knows I've got him now, Ben thought. *He'll never get even for that thrashing we gave them yesterday.*

So Ben was feeling pretty good as he made his way across the playground. Loop was smacking a ball around with a couple of class-mates, waiting for the rest of the four-square players to arrive.

"Did you guys see the paper this morning?" Ben asked.

"What paper?" Nigel replied.

"You know, with the soccer scores," Ben said.

Loop scowled. "The newspaper doesn't print the results of the Kickers League," he said.

Ben took the paper out of his pocket and

held it up. "I meant *this* paper," he said. "Let's see. The Rabbits won. But uh-oh, this Falcons score is way off. I think they got their butts kicked."

Loop rolled his eyes. Nigel grabbed the edge of the paper and looked at it, then grinned at Loop. "Guess you were a little off, huh?"

Loop shrugged. "Things didn't go our way."

Because of us, Ben thought. He laughed and started to walk away.

"Are you playing four square with us or not?" Loop asked.

"Nah," Ben said. "Not till Monday. I've got another big soccer game to get ready for. But I guess you already heard about that."

Ben held on to that good feeling throughout the day. He wasn't bothered that he only got a B on a math test. And he didn't mind that he'd forgotten to bring an extra quarter to buy a cookie at lunch. Having the upper hand on Loop for a change was all he needed right now.

He watched the clock for most of the afternoon. Larry's cross-country race was scheduled to begin at four. That would be almost as exciting as playing soccer.

*   *   *

Ben could hear a lot of yelling as he approached the park. He knew he was late, but he'd been so hungry after school that he'd run home first and eaten a peanut butter sandwich. So the race was beginning as Ben reached the park entrance.

"Go, Lincoln!" Ben yelled. He could see several green-shirted runners from Larry's team near the front of the pack as they raced across the field.

Ben had been to a couple of Larry's races here, so he knew the two-mile course. He could get a great view of the runners from the top of a hill partway through the race, then cut across this field and see them again a half mile later. From there, he'd run toward the finish line.

He saw his parents approaching, too. With

his mother working more at the bank, they were only able to get to the major sports events—like the soccer play-offs and Larry's championship races. Ben gave them a wave and scampered up the grassy hill, then made his way through the woods for about fifty yards. The runners would be coming along this trail any minute.

There were eight teams in the race, including Lincoln's biggest rival, Brookfield. The Brookfield runners were easy to spot in their red-and-black uniforms.

A small crowd of spectators was nearby. A shout went up as the lead pack of runners came into view. Larry's teammate Devin was at the front, but the group tucked tightly behind him included four runners from Brookfield and none from Lincoln.

"Come on, Devin!" Ben yelled. "You look good."

Larry was in view now, running second for Lincoln. He was usually the third or fourth runner on the team. Two of his teammates were right behind him. A steady stream of runners raced past Ben's post.

"Hold that pace!" Ben called. "Gotta catch some of those Brookfield guys."

They'd run less than a half mile, so Ben knew things would change a lot before the race was over. Larry always said it didn't matter how fast you started. The object was to *finish* strong.

Ben sprinted down the side of the hill and across the field toward a cluster of spectators who were waiting for the runners to exit the woods.

As he approached, a cheer went up. "All right, Devin!" someone yelled. "You're pulling away."

The voice sounded very familiar. Ben craned his neck to see the runners coming up the dirt path. Devin had a twenty-yard lead, but the next runner was from Brookfield. Two runners from other schools were next, then three more from Brookfield. Larry and his two teammates were several yards behind the Brookfield pack.

In cross-country, a team's first five runners score points. Unlike in most sports, the *lowest* score wins. The winner of the race scores one point for the team, second place gets two, and so on.

"Do it, Larry!" came that same voice, and this time Ben recognized it. Why was Loop at the race?

As Larry ran by, he appeared more comfortable than the runners around him. He was running very fast but pacing himself well. The race was only half over, so he had plenty of time to move up.

From the finish line, Ben would be able

to see the last half mile of the race. He started to run in that direction.

"Wait up!" called Loop.

Ben slowed a little. "What are you doing here?" he asked.

"My cousin is on the girls' team," Loop said. "Your brother looks really good today."

"He's primed," Ben said. "Very *focused*."

"I hear you," Loop said. "I guess it runs in the family."

That sounded like a compliment. But Ben could think about that later. The Lincoln runners needed to pass a few people or they'd be sorry.

"Let's go, Lincoln!" Ben yelled, although the runners were probably too far away to hear.

Ben ran toward the finish line, which was on the other side of the big grassy field.

"This way," Loop said.

"Where?"

"We'll catch them about two hundred yards from the finish," Loop replied. "That's where they need a boost, not at the finish line."

"Good call," Ben said. He followed Loop to where the runners would cut behind a baseball diamond. From there, it would be a straight sprint to the end.

They stood to the side, out of the runners' path but close.

"Should be here any minute," Loop said.

"Yeah. I didn't know you liked cross-country."

"I love to run."

"You gonna switch to cross-country in junior high?"

Loop shrugged. "Who knows? Soccer, cross-country . . . I might even play football."

"Yeah." There were a lot of sports to choose from. But they wouldn't be in junior high for three more years.

Loop was obviously in better spirits this afternoon. Ben wished he hadn't made a big deal about the soccer game at recess. Ben had played a great game—why rub it in? Loop was a terrific athlete, but nobody could win all the time.

"Here's Devin," Loop said, pointing to a spot a hundred yards away.

It appeared that Devin would win the race. He had a big lead on the first Brookfield runner. Then came a runner in a blue jersey and one in orange. Those four were spread out.

A roar came from the spectators as the next group came into view. Three red jerseys and three green ones.

"That's the whole race right there!" Loop said. "Whichever team toughs it out most will win."

As they rounded the last turn, Larry moved slightly ahead of the others in his pack.

"Sprint!" Ben yelled.

"Don't look back!" shouted Loop, jumping into the air.

As Larry passed them, Ben could barely speak from excitement. The five runners behind Larry were starting to sprint, too. Ben could hear Larry's breathing and see the pain on his face. But Larry kept going, and he was pulling away from the others.

"Think we'll win it?" Ben asked.

"Too close to call," Loop said. "But Larry looks great. They won't catch him. . . . Quite a week for your family, huh?"

Ben and Loop ran to the finish area and found Larry walking slowly with two of his teammates.

"Way to be," Loop said. "Real guts."

Larry nodded. "Thanks," he whispered.

"You all right?" Ben asked.

Larry forced a smile. "I'm wiped out. But fifth overall and second guy on the team. I'll take it."

They waited anxiously for the announcement of the team scores. Finally it came:

"Third place, with eighty-two points, Emerson."

"In second place . . ."

Ben felt his fists tighten. Lincoln was either first or second.

"Brookfield, with forty."

A big cheer went up from the Lincoln team. They'd won the title.

"The new team champion is Lincoln, with thirty-eight points."

"Awesome," Larry said, slapping hands with his teammates. He turned to Ben.

"Just another race?" Ben asked with a big grin.

Larry shook his head and beamed. "Best race I ever ran." He picked up his sweat suit and wiped his forehead with the shirt. "Think you can make it two championships in one house tomorrow?"

Ben nodded confidently. He jutted his thumb toward Loop. "The hardest part was beating this guy's team yesterday."

"Don't be too sure," Loop said. "The Rabbits are very good."

"Will you be there?" Ben asked.

"I wouldn't miss it," Loop said. "And I'll be pulling for you guys. Any team that can beat us like that deserves to win the title."

CHAPTER SEVEN
On the Run

Ben woke extra early on Saturday and quietly made his way down to the kitchen. The floor was cold on his bare feet.

He looked out the back window at the yard. Most of the leaves had fallen from the trees, and the lawn was no longer bright green.

The game wasn't until nine, so Ben hoped things would warm up by then. He couldn't wait, even though that uneasy pregame feeling was haunting him again. *Championship jitters,* he thought. But this time he was sure the nervousness would go away once the game began.

Larry came bounding down the stairs in his green sweat suit. "Feel like running?" he asked.

"I'll run plenty later," Ben said. "Aren't you tired?"

"Coach always says to run the morning after a race." Larry opened the refrigerator and took out the orange juice. "Otherwise your muscles get stiff."

Ben stuck his head inside the door, too. He grabbed a container of yogurt.

"Sleep good?" Larry asked.

"Mostly. Woke up in the middle of the night and couldn't stop thinking about the game. It's tough coming back just two days later. In the regular season, we had a week between games."

Larry laughed. "And every week, you could barely sit still waiting for Saturday. You said you would play a soccer game twice a day if they'd let you."

"Yeah. Well, this is different. It's for the title."

Larry tied his running shoes and went out the door. Ben stared at the yogurt container, then put it back in the refrigerator. He ate crackers and peanut butter instead.

The soccer field was damp with dew, and the sky was overcast and gray. But the grass had been re-marked with sharp white lines, and a table near the bleachers held shiny trophies for the winning team.

"Can you play?" Ben asked Shayna, who had warmed up with the team but was still limping.

"Maybe some," Shayna said. "It's better, but it's still sore."

"We'll use her a little at a time," Coach said. "Whenever somebody needs a breather."

That won't be me, Ben thought. *This is for the title—I definitely won't run out of steam.*

The Bobcats had lost to the Rabbits twice. The first loss was in the second game of the season, when the Bobcats were still learning to play like a team. The second time, they'd lost by a narrow 3–2 score. And they'd played that game without Ben, who'd been suspended because of a harsh penalty.

As they took the field for the championship game, he was certain the Bobcats had become the better team.

Ben and Mark were lined up on defense. "Cover the entire field," Ben said to Mark. The Rabbits played a wide-open style of soccer, bringing all of the players except the goalie forward when they had the ball. Ben and Mark planned to play the same way.

"Lots of action," Ben continued. "We have to run like never before."

Erin, Jordan, and Omar were on the front line for the Bobcats, with Kim in goal. Ben looked over at the bleachers and caught his father's eye. They pointed at each other and Ben gave a serious nod.

Everyone seemed excited. But things started badly for the Bobcats.

First Jordan tripped over the ball and fell flat on his face when he could have had a breakaway. Nothing like that had happened to him in weeks.

Then Erin made a pass directly to one of the Rabbits when Omar was wide open on her other side.

"We're in *blue*," Ben said with a laugh the

next time Erin came downfield. "Those purple guys are Rabbits."

Finally, instead of clearing the ball up the sideline, Mark made a foolish pass directly to the front of the Bobcats' goal. After some scrambling around, the Rabbits managed to score.

Mark stood with his hands clasped behind his neck, staring at the sky. "How did I do that?" he asked Ben as the teams lined up again. "That's one of the first things Coach taught us *not* to do."

"We'll settle down," Ben said. "We've been behind before. We'll get a quick goal and it'll be like starting over."

But then it was Ben who made a mistake, getting far upfield on the attack before the Bobcats had moved the ball past midfield. With Jordan dribbling along the sideline, Ben saw an opportunity to overload the offense.

But before he could set up near the goal, the Rabbits stole the ball and quickly took it the other way.

Only Mark was back on defense, and the Rabbits had a three-on-one break. Some rapid passing set up an easy shot, and suddenly the Rabbits had a 2–0 lead.

"Sub!" called Coach Patty. She waved to Ben to come off the field, and Darren ran on to take his place.

"We're not thinking," Ben said as he joined Shayna and the coach on the sideline.

"No one's playing smart," Shayna added.

"It's like we forgot how to be a team," Ben said, shaking his head.

"We don't seem to have our usual energy," Coach said. Then she laughed and turned to Ben. "Except for you. You showed a little *too* much energy out there. I'm always glad to see defenders get involved in the offense, but you

85

can't leave our end of the field unprotected like that."

Ben nodded slowly. "Looked like a real chance. Jordan's usually very reliable. . . . Didn't think he'd lose the ball."

Ben took a seat on the bench and picked up his water bottle. He unscrewed the cap and took a swig, but he wasn't thirsty yet. He let the water drip out of his mouth into the dirt.

Loop had come over and sat next to Ben. "What's going on?" he asked. "You guys look like beginners out there."

Ben kicked gently at the dirt. "I don't know."

"Listen, I can see the difference from the bleachers," Loop said. "The Rabbits are just hustling more. They're getting to every loose ball. . . . Guess we took it all out of you."

Maybe that was it. The Rabbits had played

a rather easy game in their semifinal, but the Bobcats had fought down to the final second of theirs. So no wonder Ben's team was feeling flat. They'd used up a lot of emotion in their victory.

Ben nodded. "This could get ugly."

"Yeah, if you guys let them score again, it'll be out of reach. You need to regroup and start battling harder. Slow them down a little or they'll keep scoring."

Loop held out his fist and Ben pounded it with his own. "Can I get back in there?" he called to the coach.

"Next stop," Coach said. "Give Omar a break."

On the next throw-in, Ben ran onto the field. "Just like we used to," he said to Erin and Jordan. "Smart passing, quick moves."

The Bobcats played better for the rest of the

half, and the Rabbits didn't score again. But it was still 2–0 at halftime, and the Bobcats hadn't taken a single shot at the goal.

"Twenty minutes," Ben said as they walked off the field. "That's all the time we have left to prove that we can be champions."

CHAPTER EIGHT
Gaining Momentum

"Man, I haven't played that badly since the beginning of the season," Jordan said, shaking his head and adjusting one of his shin guards. He and Ben were sitting on the bench, waiting to take the field for the second half.

Jordan had become a top scorer for the Bobcats, and he was skilled at moving with the ball and passing. But he'd made some big mistakes today.

"We played better the last few minutes," Ben said. "But we don't look like champions."

Jordan stood and stretched. "Well, I'm not going down without a fight. They might have to peel me off the field when this is over, but I'm going to run like crazy for the next twenty minutes."

"I'm with you," Ben said. He smiled slightly. "Maybe you'd better give another pep talk."

Jordan looked embarrassed, but he stood up on the bench and waved the rest of the Bobcats over. He was a quiet kid, but he'd managed to inspire his teammates at halftime of last week's game with a few choice words.

"The only difference in the first half was that the Rabbits wanted it more," he said. "They out-hustled us and they out-smarted us. We have to dig way deeper in this second half. It isn't just energy, it's *pride*. Do we have enough of it?"

"Yeah," said Mark.

"Oh, come on," Jordan said. He raised his arms high. "Do we have enough *pride?*"

"Yes!" they all said.

"Louder."

"Yes!" they shouted.

"All right." Jordan stepped down from the bench. "Let's prove it."

They ran onto the field and took their spots. Jordan, Kim, and Ben were on the front line. They'd worked well together all season, combining for quite a few goals. They'd have to be at their very best in the second half.

Ben looked across at the Rabbits' two best players. The boy was the shortest player on the team, but he was one of the best dribblers in the league. The girl with the brown ponytail was tall and fast. She'd scored goals in both previous games against the Bobcats.

Ben put the ball in play, sending a short pass

to Kim. She passed the ball backward to Erin.

Ben broke down the sideline, trying to get open.

Erin kicked the ball high in the air toward the corner. Ben sprinted toward it, arriving at the same time as that shortest Rabbit. They battled for the ball, and Ben took control. He tried to cut toward the goal, but the defender stayed right at his side.

Drop this guy, Ben told himself. *Fake him out.*

As he reached the corner, Ben turned sharply and tried to drive the ball toward the front of the goal. But the defender blocked the pass and the ball rolled over the end line.

"Corner kick!" called the referee.

Ben ran to the ball and picked it up, placing it inside the corner arc. Jordan and Kim packed in near the goal, with Erin and Mark several feet back.

Ben stepped forward and lofted the ball toward the goal. A flurry of leaping blue- and purple-shirted players darted at it.

Ben ran onto the field, and suddenly the ball was coming back to him. He'd be shooting from a tight angle, but the path between him and the goal was open. He planted his left foot and drove his right one into the ball, sending it on a line drive toward the upper corner.

The goalie jumped and stretched out his arms, catching the ball and falling to the turf. Ben sprinted back down the field.

"Good start!" Jordan called. "Let's keep up that pressure."

"Turn!" came a shout from the sideline. Shayna was pointing toward the Rabbits' goal.

Ben pivoted and shot back up the field. Erin had made a steal and was about to shoot.

The goalie knocked down the shot, but the ball rolled to the corner. This time Ben was several yards ahead of that short defender, and he got to it first. He kicked the ball with the inside of his foot, lifting it into the air and sending it to the front of the goal.

Kim was waiting. She skillfully met the ball with her forehead, driving it into the net. The Bobcats were only one goal behind.

"All right!" Ben called, racing over. "Great head."

"Beautiful pass," Kim said, slapping Ben's hands.

"Now we've got the momentum," Jordan said. "Let's keep it up."

The pace stayed at a high level after that, with both teams working hard to try to score. Ben was sweating despite the cool weather, and his legs were getting tired. But this game meant too much to let up.

Twice the Bobcats brought the ball deep into the Rabbits' zone before losing it out of

bounds. Twice more the Rabbits made a strong attack on the Bobcats' goal, only to have Darren make nice saves.

But much of the game was played near the center of the field, with both teams battling for control and neither keeping the ball for long.

Ben could hear his brother and his parents shouting along with the other spectators. They usually stayed fairly quiet during the games, but even they were more excited than usual.

After another long, hard sprint up the field, Ben stood with his hands on his knees, puffing. The ball had gone out of bounds, and they were waiting for Kim to retrieve it.

"Sub!" called Coach Patty. Ben turned and looked. Shayna was jogging onto the field and pointing at Ben. She hadn't played at all.

"Me?" Ben asked.

"Just a quick one," Shayna said.

Ben stepped off the field and walked toward the coach. She clapped her hands and said, "Great hustle."

Ben dropped to his knees and shut his eyes for a second.

"You'll recover quickly," Coach said. "You always do."

Ben nodded and said, "I'm already recovered. You can put me back in."

"Next whistle," Coach said. "There's about five minutes left in the game, so don't ever let up."

Ben stood and watched the action. Shayna couldn't move very quickly, but she didn't seem to be in much pain.

"She wanted to play a little, since this is the last game," Coach said. "But I told her to stay out of the scuffles. Just get on the field and then get off."

Mark knocked the ball out of bounds, and Coach yelled, "Sub!" again.

Ben slapped hands with Shayna as she jogged off. She had a big smile. The spectators gave her a round of applause.

He'd rested for only about a minute, but Ben felt fresh again. He darted over to the tall girl with the brown ponytail, who was moving the ball down the field for the Rabbits.

As Ben approached, she stepped over the ball and swiftly changed direction. Ben had seen that move before. He lunged forward and got his foot on the ball, knocking it to the side. Both players ran toward it, and Ben managed to get control. He fired the ball to Kim, who was yelling, "Support!"

As the ponytailed girl ran at Kim, Ben took some fast steps up the field. Kim passed to him, and Ben took off up the middle.

He'd learned to make some tricky moves as

he ran with the ball, and he needed to make them now. Two Rabbits were closing in on him. He leaned to his left, then kicked the ball to his right with the outside of his foot. That was enough to get him past the first defender, and his speed was enough to get by the second one.

Ben had an open path to the goal now, but several Rabbits were chasing him. The goalie had stepped forward, and Ben would have a hard time shooting the ball past him. Ben was near the edge of the field. He'd need some help.

A few more strides brought him close to the corner. From the side of his vision, he could see Kim moving toward the goal. He knew Jordan would be there, too.

Ben stopped short and set his foot on top of the ball to stop it. The first Rabbit stumbled past, creating a brief opening. Ben took it. He sent the ball sharply across the grass to Kim, who touched it once and nudged it ahead into Ben's path.

Ben raced to the ball. The goalie was crouched in front of him, waiting for the shot.

No way, Ben thought. He'd never slip the ball into the goal from this angle. Instead he

rolled it to the side, hoping Kim or Jordan would reach it first.

Jordan did. He booted the rolling ball directly into the net, past the diving goalkeeper.

What a comeback! The Bobcats had fought back from two goals behind and tied the score.

The Rabbits looked stunned as Kim, Jordan, and Ben ran past them. They'd had this game locked up. Now all of the momentum was with the Bobcats.

"One more!" Ben said firmly. "Next goal wins."

Jordan punched his fist into his palm. Kim jumped up and down. Ben glared at the Rabbits and let out his breath hard.

Just one more.

CHAPTER NINE
Last Chance

As the Rabbits moved down the field, Ben tried to stay aware of their two best players. *Get that ball*, he thought. *Time is running out*.

Coach had said that there would be an overtime period if the game ended in a tie. But Ben wanted to end it *now*. The Bobcats had taken control of the game.

When Mark stole the ball and headed up-field, Ben felt a rush of excitement. Things had really been clicking for the Bobcats in the past few minutes. They were ready to score again.

Mark passed to Kim, and Kim passed to Jordan. With a quick burst of speed, Jordan brought the ball deep into the Rabbits' zone. Ben was running toward the goal, too.

Jordan passed to Kim and she shot. The ball hit the goalpost and bounced to Ben's side of the field. He ran toward it with two Rabbits at his side.

Ben reached the ball and lowered his shoulder to guard it from the defenders. The short kid was to his left, and another Rabbit was between Ben and the goal. A third was approaching. He was trapped.

There was no way Ben could get the ball to the goal. He saw Erin running up from her defensive position. It would be a long backward pass, but she was open. Ben kicked it toward her.

Ben was off balance and his pass was awkward. His foot hit the turf first, and he kicked the ball with the side of his toe. The ball rolled toward the sideline.

Bad pass! Ben told himself.

The ponytailed girl swooped over and took the ball, running at full speed. She dodged past Erin into the clear. Ben chased after her.

Since the rest of the Bobcats had been near the Rabbits' goal, the girl had plenty of room to run. She crossed midfield and ran deep into the Bobcats' end of the field.

Ben and the others ran desperately back, but so did all of the Rabbits. The girl made a soft pass to the front of the goal, and the leading runner pounded it past Darren and into the net.

The Rabbits swarmed the goal scorer, yelling and jumping. They didn't just have the momentum now, they had the lead.

And the game was almost over.

Ben couldn't believe what had happened. The Bobcats had done everything right until he'd made that awkward pass.

He kicked the ball into play and chased after it. They still had a chance.

But Jordan had the ball stolen, and the Rabbits went on the attack again. Mark finally got it back and kicked it up the field, but the referee blew his whistle. "Game over!" he called.

Ben dropped to his knees and stared at the ground. He looked up to see the Rabbits at the sideline, giving each other hugs and high fives. The girl with the ponytail was bouncing side to side in a dance.

Jordan was sitting on the turf about ten yards from Ben. His mouth was hanging open as if he couldn't believe what had happened. Kim was walking slowly toward the bench. Erin was walking behind her, head down.

Coach Patty was clapping her hands and calling the Bobcats over. "Great job," she was saying. "Absolutely fantastic."

But Ben didn't feel fantastic. They'd come so close to winning the championship. They *should* have won it, as far as he was concerned.

The soccer ball was sitting on the turf a few feet away. Ben gave it a halfhearted kick toward the bench.

Coming close isn't worth anything, he

thought. *It'll be a long time before I feel like playing sports again.*

He felt a hand on his shoulder. It was Larry. "You couldn't have played any harder."

"Thanks," Ben said softly. "Could have played *better*, though."

"Nah, you were great. You coming home with us?"

"No, I'll walk. I feel like being alone to think this one over."

"I hear you. Don't worry, it won't hurt for long."

Ben watched the Rabbits receive their trophies. He put on his sweatshirt and sat on the bench, staring out at the field until nearly everyone had left. He wasn't too sad and he wasn't too angry. But he was a little bit of both. And he definitely didn't feel like talking to anyone.

So close, he thought. *One or two different*

bounces and those trophies would have been ours.

"Quite a game."

Ben turned and saw Loop walking toward him with a grin.

Ben's first reaction was to turn the other way, but then he thought again. Loop was one of the few people who could understand how Ben was feeling right now. Just two days ago, Loop had been the one who fell short.

"Great playing," Loop said, extending his hand.

Ben bit down on his lip and nodded. He shook Loop's hand. "Was it?"

"Yeah. Great *season*, too."

Ben thought that over for a second. Despite the loss, this soccer season had been one of the best experiences of his life.

"Glad it's over?" Loop asked.

Ben shrugged. "I don't know. Wish we could play that game again. I'd make sure we wouldn't start out so slow. We'd definitely beat them if we had another chance."

Loop laughed. "That's what I kept telling myself after you beat us in the semifinal. All those near misses that could have been goals . . . but you don't get another chance. You have to take your chances when you have them."

"So, what's next?" Ben asked.

Loop took a sheet of paper from his pocket and unfolded it. "Look here," he said. "Sign-ups for the basketball league at the YMCA. You up for that?"

Ben looked the paper over. "Definitely," he said.

"Maybe we can get on the same team for a change," Loop said. "That would be something, huh?"

"Yeah, it would."

The soccer ball he'd kicked toward the

bench was a few feet away. Ben picked it up and started dribbling with his hand, as if it was a basketball. Loop reached for it, but Ben shielded it with his body. He ran up the field with Loop chasing him.

Ben stopped and shot the soccer ball at an imaginary basket. "Swish!" he yelled as the ball arced through the air.

Ben looked around the field. The sun had finally broken through the clouds, and the air had warmed nicely. It would be a great afternoon for a run or a football game or basketball.

"Can you come out this afternoon?" Ben asked.

"Sure thing. Let's get some other kids. Have some kind of basketball tournament or something."

"Good deal. You'd better be ready to run."

"I'm always ready for that," Loop said with

a big smile. He picked up the soccer ball and started walking toward the goal. "Maybe we can replay that penalty kick. Let me get even."

Ben laughed. "No way. Like you said, you have to make the most of your chances when you get them. No do-overs."

"All right," Loop said. "But watch out in basketball. I've got some good moves."

"Thought we were going to be on the same team?"

"You never know. Either way. On to the next sport. And then the one after that."

Ben looked back at the soccer field as they left the park. His first real sports season was behind him now. Second place in the league was a pretty good start. He could accept that. He could be proud of it.

Especially since there were so many sports seasons ahead.

BEN'S TOP TEN TIPS FOR SOCCER PLAYERS

• Always warm up before a game or practice. Try some jogging and jumping jacks.

• Keep the ball close to your feet when you dribble. Don't just kick it and chase it.

• Pass the ball. It's the best way to move it. After you pass, move to an open space so the ball can be passed back to you.

• Sometimes the most effective pass will go backward.

• Be a supportive teammate. Say positive things and encourage everyone to work hard.

• If you usually kick the ball with your right foot, try using your left. You'll be harder to stop if you can use both feet.

• Talk to your teammates on the field, letting them know when you're open. Call "Trailing" or "Support" if you're coming up from behind, for example.

• Pass to a player who has space to work with, not one who is tightly guarded by an opponent.

• Keep control of your emotions. Getting angry or frustrated won't help you play better.

• The most important rule: Have fun!

RICH WALLACE is the much-acclaimed author of many books for young readers, including *Sports Camp; Perpetual Check; Wrestling Sturbridge*, an ALA Top Ten Best Book for Young Adults; *Shots on Goal*, a *Booklist* Top 10 Youth Sports Book; and the Winning Season series. He coached soccer for several years, beginning when his older son joined a team in kindergarten.

Rich Wallace lives in New Hampshire with his wife, author Sandra Neil Wallace. You can visit him on the Web at RichWallaceBooks.com.

Riley Liston feels like the smallest kid at sports camp. Maybe because he is. It's hard enough for a shrimp like Riley to fit in, but he just doesn't want to end up as the weak link as his bunk (the Cabin 3 Threshers) competes for the Camp Olympia trophy.

When it comes to speed-and-endurance events like running and swimming, Riley's better than he looks. He's pretty sure he can place in the top ten in the final, mile-long swim race across Lake Surprise. But he doesn't count on spotting Big Joe, the giant vicious snapping turtle of camp lore. Wasn't the lake creature supposed to be a legend?

"Exciting, tightly written sports passages drive the story and will keep kids turning the pages."
—*Booklist*

FIRST YEARLING!

Looking for more great beginner books to read? Check these out!

- ❑ *Gooney Bird Greene* by Lois Lowry

- ❑ *How Big Is a Foot?* by Rolf Myller

- ❑ THE KIDS OF THE POLK STREET SCHOOL SERIES by Patricia Reilly Giff

- ❑ *A Mouse Called Wolf* by Dick King-Smith

- ❑ NATE THE GREAT SERIES by Marjorie Weinman Sharmat

- ❑ OLIVIA SHARP: AGENT FOR SECRETS SERIES by Marjorie Weinman Sharmat

- ❑ ZIGZAG KIDS SERIES by Patricia Reilly Giff